MARC BROWN

ARTHUR'S BACK-TO-SCHOOL SURPRISE

A
Step 2
Sticker Book

D0249334

Random House 🏠 New York

Copyright © 2002 by Marc Brown. All rights reserved under International and Pan-American Copyright Conventions. Published in the United States by Random House, Inc., New York, and simultaneously in Canada by Random House of Canada Limited, Toronto.
www.randomhouse.com/kids
Library of Congress Cataloging-in-Publication Data
Brown, Marc Tolon. Arthur's back-to-school surprise / Marc Brown. p. cm. "Step into reading sticker books."
SUMMARY: Arthur is in for some embarrassing moments after he, D.W., and their mother shop for school supplies and end up buying two identical backpacks.
ISBN 0-375-81000-5 (trade) — ISBN 0-375-91000-X (lib. bdg.)
[1. Embarrassment—Fiction. 2. First day of school—Fiction. 3. Backpacks—Fiction.
4. Brothers and sisters—Fiction. 5. Aardvark—Fiction.] I. Title.
PZ7.B81618 Aokf 2002 [E]—dc21 2001048293
Printed in the United States of America First Edition July 2002 10 9 8 7 6 5 4 3 2 1
STEP INTO READING, RANDOM HOUSE, and the Random House colophon are registered
trademarks of Random House, Inc.
ARTHUR is a registered trademark of Marc Brown.

It was back-to-school time!

"I need this 3-ring binder

and the Bionic Bunny pen,"

said Arthur.

"I need these big crayons,"

said D.W.

"And you both need new shoes,"

said Mom.

SHOES

liked the first pair
that he tried on.

tried on shoe after shoe.

"I like these," she said at last.

Then D.W. got a  yellow coat
with a hood and lots of buttons.

Arthur got a

wit   written on it.

"I need a backpack,"
said Arthur.
He picked a Bionic Bunny one.
"I need one too," said D.W.
"You don't need backpacks
in nursery school," said Arthur.
"I need one to take
Mary Moo-Cow to school,"
she said.
"You can't take
that silly talking cow to school!"
said Arthur.

Mom sighed.

"Okay, D.W., pick one," she said.

D.W. picked one.

"Hey!" said Arthur. "It's the same as mine. You can't do that!"

"Why not?

I like Bionic Bunny too,"

said D.W.

Arthur picked up a backpack
with little ducks on it.

"This one is nice," he said.

"That's for babies," said D.W.

"I want Bionic Bunny."

Mom sighed.

"Oh, let her have it," she said.

"D.W. always gets her way,"
Arthur mumbled.

PAUL'S
SHOES

When they were leaving,

Mom saw a sign:

BOYS' UNDERPANTS SALE!

"You need some new underpants,"

she said, and held up a pair.

"Mom, please!" groaned Arthur.

Just then Francine stepped off

the escalator.

"Hi, Arthur," she giggled.

"Doing your

back-to-school shopping?"

Arthur was so embarrassed!

BOYS' UNDERPANTS SALE!

The first day of school,
Arthur put all of
his school things
into his backpack
and set it on the chair
by the back door.

D.W. put Mary Moo-Cow
into her backpack and set it on
the floor by the back door.

"We need to hurry," said Mom.

"Finish your breakfast
while I get the car."

"Arthur, can I see
your new classroom?" asked D.W.

"No way!" said Arthur.

"My friends will be there."

"Please," said D.W.

"N-O! Come on. We're late," he said.

Honk, honk went the car horn.

"Hurry up!" called Mom.

D.W. grabbed the backpack

on the chair

and ran out the door.

Arthur grabbed

the other backpack

and ran out too.

Arthur went to
his new classroom.
Most of his friends
were already there.
"Hi, Arthur," they said.
He unzipped his backpack
and out fell Mary Moo-Cow!
"School is fun!"
said Mary Moo-Cow.
"Can you spell fun?"

Everyone turned and
looked at Arthur.
They all laughed.
"Oh, look," said Muffy.
"Arthur brought
his favorite toy for show-and-tell!"
"Are you going to show us
your new underpants too?"
asked Francine.
Arthur covered his eyes.
He turned red.
He wished he could disappear.
Just then D.W. ran
into the classroom.

"Arthur, give me my backpack!
Here! I got yours by mistake,"
she giggled.
"And I got to see
your new classroom. So there!"
"I'll get you for this!" said Arthur.